Let's make a garden

Written and illustrated by
Tamara Awad Lobe

HERALD PRESS
Waterloo, Ontario
Scottdale, Pennsylvania

to my family, who planted my garden,
and to greg, who helped it to grow

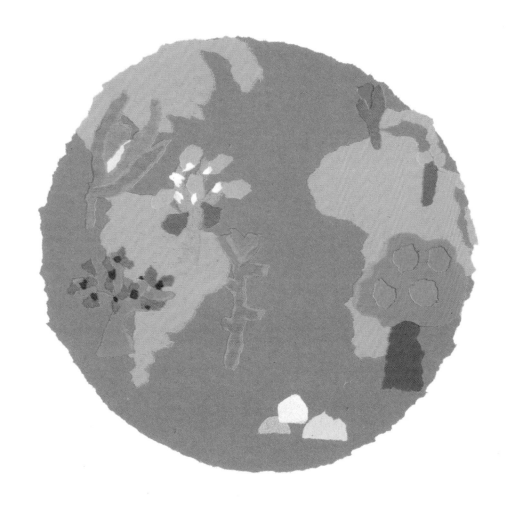

Let's make a garden! A garden of the world!

Children from all over the world can help.
What can you bring to the garden?

"I'll bring a rice plant,"
said Xiau Liu from China.

"And I'll bring an orange tree,"
said Tumi from Swaziland.

"I'll bring some spice plants,"
said Nirmala from India.

"I'll bring maize seeds," said Ikwe from the Ojibway people of Canada.

"And I'll bring rocks," said Sadako from Japan.
"Why rocks?" asked Ikwe. "You'll find out,"
Sadako said with a smile.

"We need some color," said Hans from Holland. "I'll bring tulips."

"And I'll bring beans," said
Juan from Mexico.

"We need some wheat," said
Helga from Russia.

"And I'll bring potatoes," said Julie
from the United States.

"I like olives," said Muhammed from Palestine. "I'll bring an olive tree."

"We need something sweet," said Margarita from
Costa Rica. "I'll bring a cacao tree."

What a strange combination of plants,
they thought. Where do we begin?

"I know," said Sadako. "We'll use my rocks to make the border." They all began to put the rocks in place.

And they began to dig up the land.

They put the rice in a special corner
with lots of water.

The olive, orange, and cacao trees were planted
the middle, and the tulips were put
in a circle around them.

On one edge went the spice plants, and
on the other the potatoes.

The maize, the wheat, and the beans
grew everywhere else.

The children were full of excitement,
but now they had to wait.

So they waited.

And waited.

And waited.

Many days

and many nights.

Until one day they decided they had waited
long enough. All the children got together
and went out to their garden.

And they started picking,

and picking,

and picking.

Until every basket was filled. Then they were
ready to have a HUGE PARTY!

They cooked the rice, potatoes, and beans
with the spices from India.

The maize and wheat were
ground for bread.

The cacao beans were also ground up, to
be put in milk (which all the parents
sent with the children).

The oranges and olives were put in separate baskets,
to be nibbled on later.

After all this was done, the children sat down
on a rock from Sadako, held a tulip
from Hans, and smiled.

And Xiau Liu, Tumi, Nirmala, Ikwe, Sadako, Hans,
Juan, Helga, Julie, Muhammed, and Margarita
said, "I can't wait for next year!"

About the author

Tamara Awad Lobe was born in Bluffton, Ohio, to a German mother and Palestinian father. She has traveled to many parts of the world and holds a degree in peace and conflict studies from Conrad Grebel College in Waterloo, Ontario.

Tamara and her husband, Greg, have accepted an assignment in Egypt with Mennonite Central Committee, where they will teach English as a second language.

Canadian Cataloguing in Publication Data

Lobe, Tamara Awad, 1972-
    Let's make a garden
ISBN 0-8361-9021-1
I. Title
PZ7.L63Le 1995   j813.54   C95-931914-X

The paper used in this publication is recycled and meets the minimum requirements of the American National Standard for Information Sciences—Permanence of Paper for Printed Library Materials, ANSI Z39.48-1984.